D1310046

Dedicated to our heroes- all NICU nurses, doctors, therapists and staff who provide care to the tiniest and most fragile humans. Especially the team at Saint Joseph Hospital in Denver, CO. And to Penelope Clare and Hazel Lee, my beautiful butterflies.

You girls are my everything.

— CH

Dedicated to my daughters Isabella and Iris.

— MNB

Copyright © 2021 by Carmen Hart
All rights reserved.

No part of this book may be reproduced or used in any manner without written permission of the copyright owner except for the use of quotations in a book review.

Book design by Fusion Creative Works
Book edited by Alicia Harper, Bret Hart & Victoria Fioretti
Illustrations by Mark Nino Balita www.ninobalitaillustration.crevado.com

Summary: When Penny's favorite butterfly picture goes missing in the hospital, she asks for help from her doctors, nurses and family. This beautiful tribute to prematurity is about a little girl's fierce determination and the power of love from those around her.

ISBN: 979-8-7556-1788-8

Penny and Her Butterfly

Written by Carmen Hart
Illustrated by Mark Nino Balita

When Penny was born, her mom and dad gave her a picture of a beautiful butterfly.

They told her that butterflies grow and change. After spending a long time in the cocoon, they will eventually be ready to spread their wings and soar through the world.

They put the butterfly in Penny's crib and told her that it's a reminder that she is beautiful and brave just like the butterfly. Penny loved her butterfly and she always looked at it when she wanted to feel strong. She imagined growing beautiful wings just like the butterfly and flying out of the hospital where she lived.

But, one day, Penny noticed that her butterfly was missing. "Where could it have gone?" Penny thought. She loved her butterfly and was determined to find it, so she started asking everyone if they had seen her butterfly.

First, she asked Nurse Darcrea. "Nurse Darcrea," said Penny, "You were my very
first nurse who took care of me, you must know where my butterfly is?"
"I'm sorry Penny, but I haven't seen your butterfly. Maybe you should ask
Nurse Angie because she watches over you closely at night."

"Nurse Angie, have you seen my butterfly?"

"Do you remember the last time that you saw it?" asked Nurse Angie.

"I can't remember," Penny said sadly.

"Well, that isn't helping your cause little one. But, I'll keep an eye out for it tonight. I will be sure to tell Nurse Cindy to look for it when she gets here in the morning."

"Good morning Penny Doodle. How are you today?" Nurse Cindy always had silly names for Penny to make her feel better. "Not very good, I can't find my butterfly and my butterfly helps me feel strong." Penny told Nurse Cindy. "You are the strongest little girl that I know Penny Bubbles. I'm sure that it will show up eventually. How about we tell Nurse Erin to look for it while you are sleeping tonight?" suggested Nurse Cindy.

"Hi Nurse Erin! I'm excited you are here because Nurse Cindy told me that you would help me look for my butterfly. It's disappeared, and I really miss it. You are my tallest nurse so you must be able to see everything in my room and be able to find it."

"I will look high and low tonight to try and find your butterfly Penny," said Nurse Erin.

Unfortunately, even the tallest nurse couldn't help find Penny's butterfly. Penny
knew the exact person to ask. Therapist Shannon helped her do exercises everyday.
She was always moving things around and bringing new toys into her room.
She must have seen her butterfly. "Shannon, have you seen my butterfly?"

"I'm sorry Penny," responded Shannon. "I haven't seen it, but let's ask
Nurse Krista. She might be able to help."

Nurse Krista was Penny's primary nurse, so she spent almost everyday with Penny. Penny was positive that Nurse Krista could help. "Nurse Krista, you take care of me everyday, surely you must have seen what happened to my butterfly?"

"I'm so sorry Penny, I haven't seen your butterfly, but I can tell that you are getting really tired while looking for it, so let's take a little rest and we'll be ready to look for it again later tonight with Nurse Tahlia's help."

"Nurse Tahlia, can you please help me look for my butterfly?" asked Penny.

"Of course! Have you looked in the closet? Or, by the sink?" said Nurse Tahlia.

"I've looked everywhere and I could only find my stuffed elephant, Gerry," said Penny.

"Well, there is one more nurse we can ask. Let's ask Nurse Karen tomorrow."

"Good idea," said Penny.

"Hi Penny! You look like you are getting bigger and stronger everyday. I made a blanket for you because I am so impressed by how far you have come. All of the nurses are so proud of you."

"Thanks Nurse Karen!" said Penny excitedly. Penny unfolded the blanket and shook it out in hopes that her butterfly may have been hiding in there. But, no luck.

"Daddy do you think I will ever find my butterfly?" Penny sadly asked.

"Of course I do, sweetheart. Sometimes the greatest things in this world just take a little more time to come to us. Maybe you should ask your doctors. They are the smartest people in the hospital. Maybe they know where to find your butterfly," replied Daddy.

"Hi there Penny! Do you have any questions for us today?"
asked Dr. Annie.

"Do you know when I'll be ready to go home?" asked Penny.

"Very soon," said Dr. John. "You are gaining weight and breathing very well."

"As long as you keep behaving yourself," said Dr. Mark.

"I have one more question," said Penny. "Have you seen my butterfly picture?
It's missing and no one knows where it is."

"Unfortunately, we haven't seen your butterfly Penny. But, keep working
hard little one." said Dr. Ellina.

That evening, Penny's mom was changing her crib sheets and she saw something sticking out from under the mattress. She looked closer and she realized that it was Penny's butterfly!

It had been underneath her the whole time! Penny gave her mom a big hug and was so excited to finally find her beautiful butterfly.

Penny thanked everyone for helping her find her butterfly. She was lucky to have so many amazing people helping her get bigger and stronger. After 101 days in the hospital, Penny finally turned into a butterfly herself and was able to fly home.

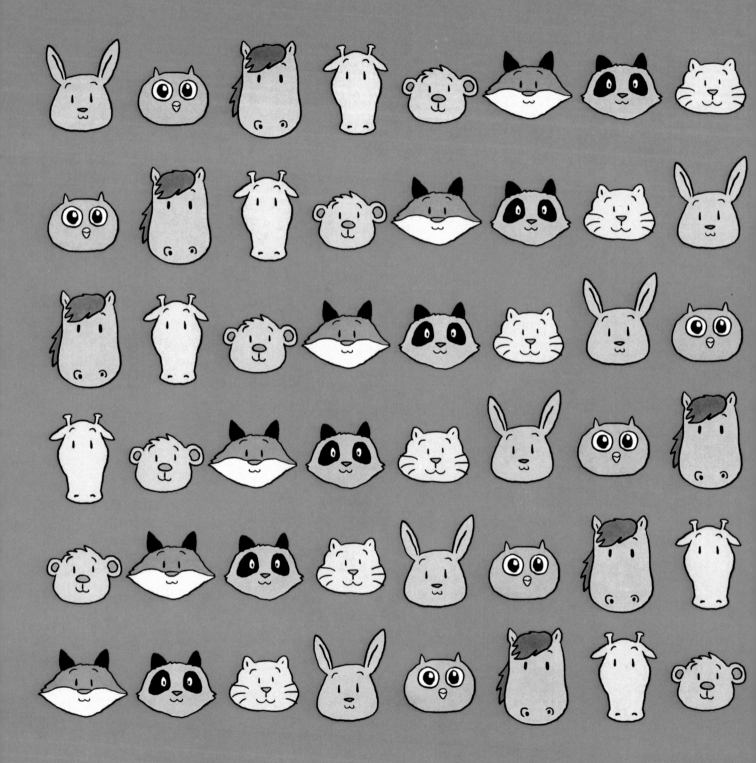

Penelope "Penny", was born at only 27 weeks on July 21, 2016. Three months earlier than expected. She is the strongest little fighter that we know and we are so proud to call her our daughter. Her NICU days were difficult, but we look back with so much pride on the amazing journey that we have been on as a family.

We are honored to donate proceeds of this book to organizations that help families, like ours. March of Dimes funds lifesaving research and programs in an effort to end premature birth. And the Saint Joseph Parent 2 Parent Support Group helps families currently experiencing a NICU stay at their hospital in Denver, Colorado. Proceeds will help these amazing organizations.

Made in United States
North Haven, CT
14 April 2022

18286553R00015